CHINESE DYNASTIES

Shang c. 1766-1027 BC ▷

Chou 1027-256 BC ▷

Ch'in 221-206 BC ▷
Western Han 202 BC-8 AD ▷
Eastern Han 25-221 AD ▷
Three Kingdoms 221-280 AD ▷
Northern and Southern Dynasties 317-589 AD ▷
Sui 589-618 AD ▷
T'ang 618-907 AD ▷
Five Dynasties 907-960 AD ▷
Northern Sung 960-1126 AD ▷
Southern Sung 1126-1279 AD ▷
Yuan 1279-1368 AD ▷
Ming 1368-1644 AD ▷
Ch'ing 1644-1912 AD ▷

TAIWAN

HONG KONG

One human being in every four lives in China, and many other people of Chinese descent are spread round the rest of the world too.

Throughout its long history, the civilisation of China has been very different from that of the West, the cultures differing in the past just as much as the politics do now.

This book is about old China, and about some of the ways that Chinese ideas and inventions have affected us despite these differences.

Acknowledgments
The map on pages 22-23 and the illustration on page 42 are both by the author, Dr I A Morrison; the front endpaper map is by Gerald Witcomb. Colour photographs on pages 15 and 17 and the cover are from the Hamlyn Group, those on pages 12, 14, 21, 24-25, 36-37, and 50-51 are from Robert Harding Associates, pages 47 and 48-49 are from Paul Popper Ltd, and the photograph on pages 18-19 is from the *Sunday Times*. The print on page 41 is from the Mansell Collection.

Great Civilisations
China

by IAN A MORRISON MA PhD

with illustrations by
ANNIE BENNETT

Ladybird Books Ltd Loughborough 1978

I. China Emerges

The Chinese call their country *Chung Kuo*, the Central Nation. In calling it China, we commemorate the Ch'in dynasty. A dynasty is a family of rulers, and the Ch'in emperors were first to unify the land in 221 BC, in the days of the ancient Greeks and Romans.

There had been other dynasties before them. The Chou went right back to the time of David and Solomon, around 1000 BC. Even before them, during the Shang dynasty (which started before Tutankhamun became king of Egypt) the Chinese were already growing wheat, living in walled cities, writing on bamboo and making silk cloth.

After the Ch'in unification, the most famous dynasties were the Han, T'ang, Sung and Ming. The Han lasted for about two centuries on either side of the life of Christ. T'ang (618–907 AD) ran from the time of the Prophet Mohammet until after Charlemagne. By then there were already as many people in China as there are in England today. Sung overlapped with the Viking voyages to Greenland and America, and with the Crusades, while Ming lasted from the 14th century on through the lifetimes of Columbus and the Pilgrim Fathers to the English Civil War.

All this time the number of Chinese people was increasing. Today the country has to support the largest population it has ever had. Besides the 700 million or so in China itself, many others live elsewhere. From Los Angeles to London we can eat Chinese food, hear Chinese spoken and see Chinese writing.

This piece of graph paper measures 100 by 100 mm, so you are looking at 10,000 little squares.

A piece of this paper just 1 metre by 1 metre would have one million of these squares.

If you wanted to represent each of the people living in China with one of the tiny squares, you would need a roll of this paper 1 metre wide by 700 metres long . . . that's nearly half a mile!

II. The Land of China

China, one of the largest countries in the world, is very varied in geography, running from the glaciers of Tibet down to the steamy delta-lands by the China Sea.

To the north are the windy plains of Manchuria and Mongolia, once homes of fierce horsemen. The cradle of Chinese civilisation lay where the climate is pleasanter and the soils are rich, along the Yellow River. Further south is a vast area of hills, plains and lakes, centred on the river Yangtze. Here the climate becomes quite tropical, and there is usually more than enough rain. Rice is the main crop, whereas wheat, millet and beans dominate in the north.

The wild forests that once grew in the centre and south have mostly gone, but to the west, jungles survive. Where these rise from the Szechwan basin of the Yangtze onto cooler ranges leading towards the Himalayas, strange animals survive too: odd goat-antelopes, golden snub-nosed monkeys, and the Giant Panda.

Pandas are only really happy eating the bamboo of the Cloud Forest there, so they find it difficult to live outside China. But the pheasant, another decorative native of Szechwan, has been introduced to North America and Europe with great success.

Their rivers have always been especially important to the Chinese. Many of the richest farmlands are made of the soil they have deposited. Some of this material started as *loess*, a fine dust blown into the air from bare lands round the glaciers during the Ice Age. This settled on China in great thicknesses. Where rivers cut canyons into it, people carved cave homes, warm in winter and pleasantly cool in summer.

The rivers also provided highways for boat travel. The Chinese linked these up with canals from early times. The Prince of Wu made the first practical inland waterway in 486 BC (just before the ancient Greeks built the Parthenon) and it is still in use as part of the Grand Canal linking Hangchow with Peking.

Working on a river dyke

Rivers also created problems. The Chinese have shown great skill in solving these. From very ancient times they made suspension bridges with bamboo cables to cross ravines. They were using iron chains to bridge 100 metre gaps by 600 A D, more than eleven hundred years before the first successful Western chain suspension bridge.

Flood control has always been their main difficulty, however. For example, each year the Yellow River, 'China's Sorrow', shifts a thousand million tonnes of the yellow mud that gives it its name. This builds up its beds above the level of the farmland, causing catastrophic floods when the banks burst. As long ago as the Ch'in dynasty, the engineer Li Ping had the right idea: 'Keep the dykes low, and dig the channel deep.' It is hard work though, even with modern dredgers.

Floods were one problem, but there were droughts too. One folktale tells how the farmers at Horse Ear Mountain were starving, their lands were so parched.

Then a peasant's daughter called Sea Girl found a secret lake shining in the mountains. The wild goose that guarded it told her that the lake could only be opened with a golden key, but didn't tell her where to find it. Three parrots sent her off to seek the Third Daughter of the Dragon King. A peacock helped by leading her to the canyons of the southern mountains, and explaining that Third Daughter liked folksongs.

Sure enough, after Sea Girl had sat singing for three days, she appeared and joined in (although her father had forbidden that kind of thing). They made friends, and when Sea Girl had explained they made a plan.

They sang very loudly together until the killer eagle who guarded the King's treasure flew over to investigate. Third Daughter kept singing to him while Sea Girl sneaked into the treasury and got the key. Since

she was good and left all the jewels, the eagle didn't notice that anything was missing. They got away all right, and unlocked the lake.

The villagers were saved, but the Dragon King was furious. He banished his daughter, who went to stay with Sea Girl.

They still like singing together. Every year on the twenty second day of the seventh month all the ladies of Horse Ear Mountain come round and join in, as a way of saying thank you.

Loess terraces

Like the lands around Horse Ear Mountain, much of China needs irrigation if the crops are to grow. Indeed over its long history China's scenery has been transformed by the work of the irrigators. In the north the wheat and the millet is grown on row upon row of carefully watered terraces cut into the loess hillsides. Even in the south where water is plentiful, the landscape has been turned into an intricate mosaic of terraced paddyfields that can be flooded whenever this is needed by the rice plants.

Planting rice

Rice is the most important food of China. It has been cultivated since prehistoric times, and some folk-tales say that it was the gift of the goddess Kuan Lin.

Other folktales say that rice was a present from a dog. These stories tell how the waters overflowed and engulfed the whole world. Yu (who was himself born a dragon) put the water back into the sea by using a dragon's tail to dig canals, and by turning himself into a bear to tunnel through mountains.

The flood had destroyed all the old plants, and men could only live by hunting, since there were no new plants.

Then one day a dog climbed out of a water-logged field, with yellow bunches of seeds hanging from his tail. The people planted these in the wet fields, and rice grew. People who believe this story always offer food to the dog before they themselves eat.

Rice-giving dog

III. Ancient Beliefs

Besides folktales such as these, the Chinese had many kinds of beliefs and religions. Some of these were brought back by their travellers and voyagers. The great Indian religion of Buddhism arrived by the 1st century AD, was changed gradually, and then in its new Chinese form spread to influence much of south-east Asia. One visible sign of this was the blending of Chinese tower-building with the Indian idea of religious mounds to produce the beautiful *pagoda*.

The main pagoda at the Summer Palace, Peking

Another religion centred on the thoughts of Confucius. He lived in China at the time of some of the ancient philosophers of Greece, around 500 BC, and like them he has continued to influence thinkers in the West as well as East into modern times. His sayings take in universal human ideals, common to many religions (for instance, 'behave to others as you would like them to behave to you'). He is also associated with the strong Chinese tradition of respect for parents and ancestors.

In old China, families often had their own gods. Little figures of them guarded the doors, and there were special kitchen gods and so on to look after each household department. In this the Chinese showed the same liking for neat organisation they expressed in their Civil Service. This was complicated but very efficient at running the country. They even liked to imagine that Heaven was run by a Celestial Civil Service, and of course Hell needed one to keep registers of who should be down there and what punishments they deserved!

A Men-Shen, or guardian of the door (household god)

The Chinese have a favourite story about a certain Monkey, who represents the forces of Disorder and Cheerful Chaos.

He started out by organising all the other monkeys into a kingdom, aiming to take over the world . . . but he got drunk, and was carried off to Hell. Down there he broke his chains and stole the Judge of Hell's register, to score off the names of all the monkeys.

Then he went aloft for a bit. But when he started to break up Heaven itself, the Heavenly Host besieged him on Mount Huakuo, twice! They captured him the second time, and the Jade Emperor condemned him to death.

They tried to melt him in an alchemist's furnace, heated to white heat for forty nine days. That didn't work, because between the two sieges he had eaten the peaches from the Heavenly Peach Garden, the source of Everlasting Life.

When he threatened to destroy Heaven altogether, the Buddha intervened and shut him inside a magic mountain. He was finally let out to help the good Thang Seng to fetch sacred Buddhist scriptures from India for China.

Before starting, Thang Seng wisely fixed a helmet on Monkey that would squeeze his head whenever he was wicked.

Monkey helped so faithfully through all the troubles of the great journey west, however, that when they got back he was forgiven for all his mischief, and the helmet disappeared.

The Judge of Hell

17

Buddha rewarded Thang Seng's horse, by turning it into a dragon and making it Chief of the Celestial Dragons. Dragons appear in lots of Chinese stories. In our own fairy tales dragons are usually fiery and nasty, but the Chinese ones live in the clouds or the waters and bring good fortune.

The word for dragon is *lung*, and there were five main kinds. Imperial Dragons, the symbol of the Emperor, had five claws on each foot. The rest were

just four-toed dragons. The Celestial or Heavenly Dragons guarded the mansions of the Gods. Spiritual ones looked after the winds and rains, and helped water the crops. They might cause flooding, but that would be an accident. The Earthly Dragons cleared rivers, deepened the seas, and helped people like Yu to control floods.

Treasure Dragons kept an eye on hidden treasure, and *they* could be nasty (unless you were the rightful owner of the treasure).

In general however dragons have meant excitement and good luck, so Dragon Kites have always been favourites with Chinese boys and girls. Dragons are often painted on pottery too. The Chinese New Year is celebrated with fireworks, while enormous paper dragons wind through the streets, carried by long chains of leaping men. This has been seen in America and England in recent years where many of the 'dragon's feet' are waiters from the Chinese restaurants.

A Chinese paper dragon in London

Floating fish-shaped iron compass, 1044 AD

A 13th century Chinese needle compass

If an Emperor was a particularly good ruler, a fabulous beast called a *Chi-Lin* might appear. It was said to be enormous but quiet and kindly, with odd horns and yellow spots. It sounded rather unlikely, and probably no one quite believed in it. That is, until some Chinese sailors brought one home! But the giraffe is indeed a quite unlikely beast . . . They had been to Africa, with Admiral Cheng Ho. This was in the early 15th century.

Few Westerners realised it at the time, but the Chinese Navy was certainly the greatest in the world for most of the period between the voyages to America of Leif Ericsson in 1000 AD and Columbus in 1492.

The earliest report of the magnetic compass, for example, came from China, and although Chinese *junks* look very different, several important parts used in Western vessels appear to have been invented first by the Chinese. These include watertight compartments to save damaged ships from sinking, and even the ordinary rudder for steering. This was in use in China by the time Julius Caesar invaded Britain, over a thousand years before it became known in the West.

By the time of Admiral Cheng Ho, their great junks could carry a thousand men, with supplies to last weeks. They sailed far north in the Pacific to fetch Siberian furs, and went west to India, Arabia, even Madagascar and the south of Africa, cutting across open oceans guided by their compasses.

A present-day junk

21

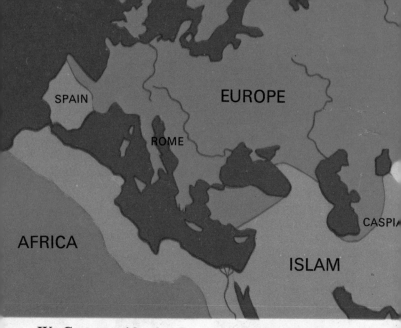

SPAIN

EUROPE

ROME

AFRICA

CASPIA

ISLAM

IV. Contacts with other Peoples – in war and peace

We tend to forget that Europe was discovered by
China, and not the other way round. Early Chinese
explorers went great distances overland too. Around
130 BC Chang Ch'ien travelled right across Asia and
found out about Europe when he came upon Greek
Bactria, a colony set up by Alexander the Great's
soldiers on the way to India.

Even in Roman times, whole armies of Chinese were
pushing far towards the west. In 97 AD one army
came as far as the Caspian Sea, in what is now Soviet
territory. When the Arabs were spreading their new
religion of Islam, they met a Chinese army carrying the
banners of the Tang dynasty westwards, and stopped

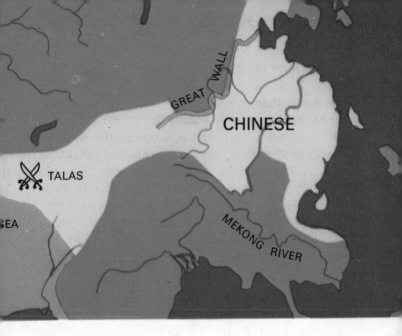

them in 751 AD at the battle of Talas, north-east of Samarkand. It is intriguing to wonder what might have happened in Western civilisation if the Chinese had won instead and taken over the Arab empire, for the Arabs were occupying Spain then and had even swept into France not long before.

Of course not all contacts were warlike, and as we shall see, Chinese trade goods reached ancient Rome. Roman coins are found in south-east Asia too. The exports and money were probably traded through many hands and, as far as we know, no Romans set up shop personally by the Mekong river, nor Chinese by the river Tiber in Italy. News and ideas very probably travelled with the goods nevertheless.

Although the Chinese might expand outwards, at home they were often in danger from raiding northerly tribes.

Sometimes these nomadic horse-warriors won. The great Mongol war-lord Kublai Khan even became Emperor of all China. Often however the Chinese were able to keep them out. To do this they developed a chain of fortifications that gradually grew into the Great Wall of China. It is some 2400 kilometres long. This is nearly *twice* the distance from London to Rome. So it makes the Roman wall across England look pretty small! It was started about 214 BC, but much of what is to be seen now dates from the Ming dynasty (mainly in the European Middle Ages).

The Chinese were wall-builders long before then, however. The Shang dynasty started around 1600 BC, when Stonehenge was still quite new in England. One Shang capital, Cheng-chou, had a city wall 7.2 kilometres long. This still stands over 9 metres high, and is up to 36 metres wide. It contains about 3 million tonnes of soil, and Chinese archaeologists think it would have taken 10,000 men nearly twenty years to build it.

By the Han dynasty, in Roman times, one imperial capital, Ch'ang-an, had 24 kilometres of city walls. For even more security, the area within these was divided into 160 wards, each with its own wall and a gate guarded at night.

The Great Wall of China

Rocket-launching equipment

By the 9th century AD Chinese alchemists were being warned not to mix certain substances that were likely to go off with a *whoosh* and singe their beards. Gunpowder was discovered, and soon rockets were being made from bamboo tubes. There followed mobile batteries of war-rocket launchers mounted on 'wooden-oxen' (wheelbarrows, which were also a Chinese invention).

By 1230 the Sung dynasty were using really spectacular explosions in their campaign against the Mongols. Within a century real cannons had appeared.

Although gunpowder seems to be a Chinese invention, nobody is quite sure whether the notion of using it in metal tubes to fire things for long distances started among the Chinese themselves, or among the Arabs, or in Europe – but it was certainly to change the course of European history.

Francis Bacon, the early English scientist, believed that the three inventions of gunpowder, printing and the magnetic compass had each changed Western history. We now believe all were first discovered by the Chinese.

Some modern historians even go further. They suggest that the horseman's stirrup was another Chinese development, and that this was literally what kept knights-in-armour in the saddle. Heavy and invincible, they dominated medieval Europe from horseback until gunpowder in its turn arrived and made their castle strongholds vulnerable.

Kublai Khan

Even some of the great conflicts had peaceful results however. When Kublai Khan made himself Emperor of China in the 13th century AD, his Mongols had conquered an enormous empire that reached all the way across Asia to the very borders of Europe. This meant that if you were on friendly terms with them, they could give you safe conduct to travel the whole way to China overland.

This is what Marco Polo did. He was an Italian from Venice. When he set out with his father Niccolo and his uncle Maffeo to travel to China, he was just sixteen years old. He was almost forty before he returned in 1294.

His book about Cathay, as he called China, became a best-seller in medieval Europe, and it is still good reading. Christopher Columbus had a copy on which

Marco Polo

he wrote careful notes, and it was while looking for a westward route to Cathay that he accidentally discovered America.

Marco's book gave Europeans an impression of the extraordinary strangeness and richness of Chinese life. He did exaggerate (he liked huge numbers, and was nicknamed *Il Milione* which means 'The Million', for this), but sometimes even he did not grasp just how impressive the things he saw in China really were. Thus, although the Chinese Grand Canal caught his attention because he was a Venetian (in Venice canals are common), he did not realise parts of it were already hundreds of years old when he saw it.

When he finally got home, he did not get much of a welcome. In fact it was to pass the time in an Italian jail that he dictated his famous book!

Some think Marco Polo brought the idea of spaghetti from China to Italy. It is mainly in the present century however that Chinese food has become such a popular element in the contact between the culture of China and the people of the West.

The chief delight of Chinese cookery is that it brings out the individual flavours and different crisp or soft textures of the foods. To achieve this, instead of stewing foods together they are often cooked and served in separate dishes. They are then eaten together, sampling a mouthful of this and of that.

One favourite way of preserving fresh flavours is to fry thinly shredded vegetables very quickly in really hot oil, forking them over continuously so that they cook right through. Seasoned Chinese dishes are good

A floating kitchen

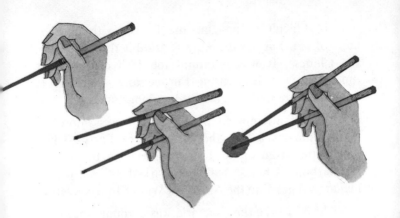

too, and most Chinese meals have at least one *red-cooked* dish, that is, one cooked in soy sauce. A traditional Manchu banquet might have as many as three hundred different dishes to choose from.

It is said that for the Chinese the line separating civilised people from barbarians was that dividing those who ate with chopsticks from those who used their fingers (or in later times, such inferior implements as knives and forks!).

The trick with chopsticks is to work them as pincers, but don't try to move both at once: keep one still. To hold that 'still' one, grip it in the V where thumb and forefinger meet, and steady it with the third finger. Then take the other chopstick between ball of thumb and forefinger, and with it pivoting there use your middle finger to move it in and out.

To wash down your food you might drink rice wine, or green tea.

It is difficult to imagine the British without their cups of tea, but tea drinking is a habit they got from the Chinese. It was not until the 18th century that much tea was brewed in Europe and America. It remained rare and expensive for a long time.

A British attempt to put up prices even more by taxing imports led to the 'Boston Tea Party', when Americans disguised as Indians threw tea boxes into the harbour. Chinese tea thus sparked off one of the incidents that led to the American War of Independence.

Right up to the time Victoria was a young queen, all the tea drunk in the world was grown in China. Soon after that other teas were grown in Assam in India and in Ceylon, but they had flavours of their own and many people have continued to prefer China tea.

Some of the fastest and most beautiful sailing ships ever built were Tea Clippers. The first ships home from China with the fresh crop from each year's harvest got the best prices, so they were designed to race. They travelled almost two-thirds of the distance round the earth, sailing heavy-laden through the East Indies, right across the Indian Ocean to the southern tip of Africa, and then up the length of the Atlantic. Yet the best sometimes did this in less than ninety days, all on wind-power without any engines. Happily one of the most famous, *Cutty Sark*, built in Scotland in 1869, has been preserved and you can go aboard her at Greenwich on the Thames below London.

A Tea Clipper, with a junk close behind

An 18th century Chinese plate decorated with Scottish Highlanders

V. Chinese Art and Science

We say that the cups from which we drink our tea are made of *china*. That we often mean the crockery rather than the country when we speak of china shows how much we have been influenced by the Chinese skill with pottery.

This influence has been expressed in different ways. The best of Chinese art pottery has been treasured by private collectors and museums in the West, but since it has always been costly, Western potteries long ago started mass-producing crockery that looked Chinese (at least to our eyes). Your grandmother probably had lots of 'Willow Pattern' china of this kind.

Realising there was a market for them in the West, during the 18th and 19th centuries Chinese potters began to turn out what *they* thought Westerners would buy. Some of this, just cheap copies of traditional Chinese designs, is rather boring. But sometimes it is quite fun . . . as when they tried their hands at painting tartan Scotsmen!

Attempts by Western craftsmen to make things look 'Chinese' sometimes worked out even more strangely. The fashion for *Chinoiserie* as it was called did not affect only textiles and furniture, it even affected the decoration of Royal Navy ships. In the early 18th century the traditional British Lion figureheads suddenly turned out like enormous Pekinese dogs . . . which must have looked a bit startling, looming out of the mist in the English Channel!

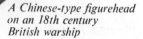

A Chinese-type figurehead on an 18th century British warship

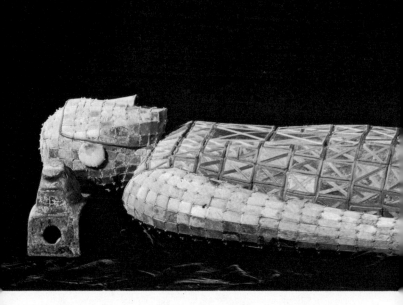

Some of the things that reached the West from China were very precious indeed. Besides some superb porcelain and pottery there were bronze vessels and jars carved from ivory or decorated with lacquer. These materials were all also used in making figures of gods, people and beasts, both real and imaginary.

Such things only reached Europe in any quantity from the 17th century onwards, but Europeans were familiar with Chinese cloth far earlier. The great caravan route through Central Asia was already bringing Chinese silks to Rome before the end of the 1st century AD, and Roman ladies made dresses out of them. Before the Middle Ages were over, cathedral robes in Poland and Austria included panels of silk

A jade princess

with pictures of Chinese birds and beasts, while Italian weavers were copying Chinese dragons and phoenixes.

One of the most highly prized of the Chinese art materials was jade. This is a very hard greenish stone that can be ground into smooth shapes, pleasant to touch. In Chinese tradition it represents five virtues:

Charity (being bright yet warm);
Trustworthiness (showing its internal colours);
Wisdom (ringing true);
Courage (occasionally broken, never bent);
Fairness (perhaps sharp, but never cutting).

Almost indestructible itself, it was believed to preserve and protect. So a dead princess was clad in a suit of jade plates, and jade carvings were carried as charms.

Another Chinese art form much admired in the West is their lettering. Many Westerners enjoy its beauty, even though they do not understand it. It is difficult for us to learn because it works quite differently from our kind of writing.

When we write a word down, we use the alphabet as a kind of code to capture the sounds that we make in saying that word. The letters of our alphabet are just signs that we learn. They are not pictures of anything in particular.

Sometimes, in things like international road signs, we do use pictures to express not sounds but meanings. Chinese writing seems to have started out that way, more than three-and-a-half thousand years ago, with actual drawings of the things represented. In these ancient *pictographs* a tree or a hill is quite recognisable. Drawings however take time, and by the Chou

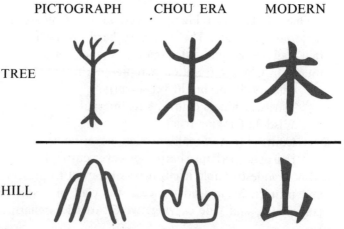

PICTOGRAPH	CHOU ERA	MODERN
TREE		
HILL		

dynasty realism was being sacrificed for marks that were quicker to make. Nowadays the process has gone so far that it would be difficult to guess that the marks were originally pictures at all.

Often, one spoken sound may have several meanings. So if we hear 'dear' in English, it may mean 'expensive' or 'someone we're fond of', or even 'deer with antlers'.

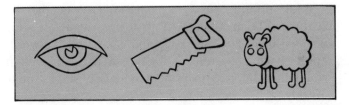

Perhaps you send code messages to your friends, using puns like this: a drawing of an eye followed by a wood-saw and then a sheep to mean 'eye saw ewe . . . I saw you'.

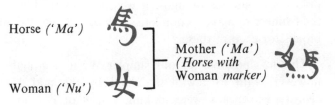

Horse ('Ma')

Woman ('Nu')

Mother ('Ma')
(Horse with
Woman marker)

This happens in Chinese too: 'Ma' means 'Horse' . . . or 'Mum'! With more than 50,000 signs to remember already, to save inventing even more they use the pun and draw the horse sign that gives the clue to the sound. But they carefully put the sign for Woman with it so that they don't get into trouble with the lady concerned!

When all books had to be written out by hand, this was so slow that very few copies were made and few people could be educated in the kind of difficult-to-memorise knowledge that books are good at storing. The invention of printing was thus very important for the emergence of the kind of civilisation that has developed in modern times.

Book printing seems to have started in the 9th century AD in China. At first they made one big wooden block for each page and carved all the words on it. Each page took a long time to make, but it could then be used to print hundreds of copies quite quickly.

By the 11th century they had the idea of making smaller blocks and clamping these together temporarily to say what they wanted. This way some blocks could be re-used in different pages. But since their writing involves thousands of signs, it was not practicable for the Chinese to make a complete stock of little individual blocks for each of these.

This *was* possible for our simpler Western alphabet however, with its few letters, and by the mid 15th century Europeans were making stocks of individual letters that they could use over and over again to spell out whatever they wished. So modern publishing was getting under way just before Columbus reached America.

Paper making had come to Europe by the 12th century. The Chinese were doing it considerably earlier, and had even invented paper money (and inflation)

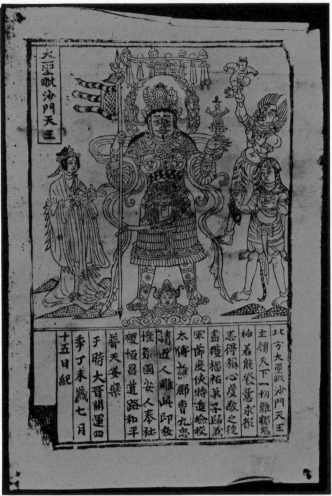

A prayer sheet printed in 947 AD, over a thousand years ago

by the 9th century. It was the 18th century before Westerners took up the Chinese fashion of decorating their homes with printed wallpapers.

A paddle-driven war junk

The development of printing helped to speed up the exchange of knowledge, but as we have seen, many ideas seem to have been interchanged between China and the West long before printing was widespread.

While it is true that good ideas get passed on, it is always difficult to be quite sure whether an invention which turns up in different places really has spread from one source, or whether different peoples have had the same useful notion independently. Sometimes what happens seems a complicated mixture, with a basic idea being shared in an unexpected way.

For example, in the 1840s in the early days of Western paddle steamers, British ships met Chinese war junks propelled by paddle wheels powered by lots of men working treadmills (like hamster exercise wheels). The Western sailors thought they were just doing their best, lacking engines, to copy the steamers. But in fact the Chinese had been using treadmill paddle wheelers ever since the last days of the Roman empire. By the period of the Crusades, there were great paddle battleships in China, with up to 23 man-powered wheels (eleven-a-side, plus one at the back like a Mississippi stern wheeler). Nobody knows whether 16th century Italian experiments with muscle-powered paddle wheels owed anything to China.

Nevertheless, an extraordinary variety of ideas do seem to have come to us from China: from kites to blast-furnaces, clock mechanisms to keystone-arch bridges, from examinations for Civil Service recruiting, to a whole range of medical knowledge.

A Chinese water clock   43

From very early times the Chinese showed great knowledge of the actual medicinal properties of fruits, herbs and minerals. This picture shows the god Shou Lao, bringing the peach that was a symbol of long life to the Chinese (as Monkey knew – see page 16).

Even some of the prescriptions attributed to the legendary Emperor Shen Nung (said to have ruled around 2700 BC, before the Pyramids were built in Egypt) are accepted by modern doctors. For example: opium as a drug; rhubarb as a purge; *kaolin* (powdered clay) to dry up a troubled stomach; and a substance called *ephedrine* for asthma. By the mid 16th century AD, when Queen Elizabeth I was a young girl, Li Shi-Chen had written a fifty two volume 'Great Herbal' describing over 1800 drugs and herbs such as those shown on the right.

The god Shou Lao

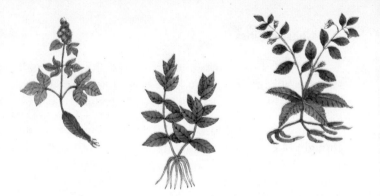

Surgery using pain killers was certainly practised in China as long ago as the ancient Greeks, and the Chinese have made use of gymnastic exercises for health purposes for centuries. *Acupuncture* (pricking the skin) may go back to Shen Nung, but some Western doctors are now interested in this for possible muscle treatments.

We tend to think of immunisation against smallpox as starting with Jenner in Britain in the 18th century, but it was done successfully in China by sniffing powdered smallpox scabs at least from the days of the first Queen Elizabeth, and indeed possibly some five hundred years earlier.

The Chinese were also early in recognising the health value of cleanliness. They used tooth-brushes, and they seem to have been first with toilet paper as well as writing paper. Sewage and refuse collecting systems reflected their understanding of the relationship between epidemics of disease and hot dirty crowded towns.

VI. Chinese Cities

Many of the Chinese have always lived in small country villages, but there have been quite large towns ever since the Shang dynasty started around 1600 BC.

By the time of Marco Polo, Hangchow (which he thought 'a city greater than any in the world') certainly had more than a million inhabitants. They ate two hundred tonnes of rice each day. Some lived in wooden multi-storey flats, and there were terrible fires. After one in 1137 had gutted 10,000 homes, a proper fire-brigade was set up.

Although the people tended to be tightly packed within the old walled cities, the traditional Chinese house gave a sense of privacy. It was centred on a courtyard often called the Well of Heaven which was always (however small) a garden with plants, little trees in pots, and perhaps a goldfish pond.

A large family house would have two courtyards. Inside the street gateway was the more public one, where business was done with passing traders. Behind was the private yard, with the rooms of the different members of the family opening off it.

The whole would be very colourful, with sweeping wide-eaved roofs of pantiles, decorated wooden beams, and walls of tinted plaster. Inside, the richer families had carved and painted furniture, and embroidered cushions and drapes.

In the cities there were busy markets and quarters

given over to all the different kinds of craftsmen. The grandest buildings were the temples and palaces, and some of the finest of these survive in Peking.

A pagoda in the famous garden of Shih Tzu Lin, in Soochow

The Imperial Palace

Peking is the capital of China. Though its name and fortunes have changed, there has been a city on its site for a very long time. Even during the Chou dynasty, at the time of the ancient Greeks, it covered 33 square kilometres.

Its earliest name was Ch'i, but it had many different names over the centuries. Kublai Khan the Mongol, whose other capital was Xanadu, named it Khanbaliq (Khan-City). Between 1260 and 1290 A D he built the first enclosed imperial city and palace at Peking. He followed the traditional Chinese grid pattern that first appeared long before at Cheng-chou. Marco Polo confirms that it resembled a chessboard with sides nearly 10 kilometres long.

The Ming dynasty who followed on from the Mongols

took over the site as capital and extended Peking south of the Mongol town.

The Forbidden City of Peking is the Imperial Palace area. It is surrounded by a rectangle of high walls and a moat, and was laid out by Yung-Lo, the third Ming Emperor. He ruled three-quarters of a century before Columbus' voyage, but many of the buildings he started can still be seen.

You enter from the south by the gate of the Mid-Day Sun, and find yourself in a city within a city, with great bronze dragons guarding the palaces and the Pearl that was the symbol of Imperial Treasure. This was intended to be the place from which all power radiated, the centre of China and of the civilised world, to be on earth what the Pole Star is in the sky.

VII. New China

Now there is a different star over China, a red one. In 1949 Mao Tse-Tung proclaimed the People's Republic of China, and the country officially became a Communist state.

Although it is little more than a quarter of a century since this happened, a tiny period against the long history of traditional .Chinese civilisation, in many ways this short time has seen more changes in the life-style of the people of China than many much longer periods in the past.

In the past however when beliefs and ideas have come into China from outside, they have generally been changed by the Chinese until they suited their own way of doing things. In this case too although changes from the old ways have been many and rapid, it seems that once again the Chinese are going their own way.

A New Zealander living in China has written recently that China '. . . ever weaves the best of its past into its present as it fights for the future.'

Children in present-day China

INDEX